THE TWELVE DAYS OF KINDERGARTEN

A Counting Book

written by
Deborah Lee Rose

illustrated by
Carey F. Armstrong-Ellis

ABRAMS BOOKS FOR YOUNG READERS • NEW YORK

On the first day of kindergarten, my teacher gave to me

the whole alphabet from A to Z.

2

On the second day of kindergarten,
my teacher gave to me
TWO picture books
and the whole alphabet from A to Z.

3 On the third day of kindergarten,
my teacher gave to me
THREE pencils,
two picture books,
and the whole alphabet from A to Z.

On the fourth day of kindergarten,
my teacher gave to me
FOUR puzzle shapes,
three pencils,
two picture books,
and the whole alphabet from A to Z.

5 On the fifth day of kindergarten,
my teacher gave to me
FIVE gold stars!
Four puzzle shapes,
three pencils,
two picture books,
and the whole alphabet from A to Z.

6 On the sixth day of kindergarten,
my teacher gave to me
SIX fish for feeding,
five gold stars!
Four puzzle shapes,
three pencils,
two picture books,
and the whole alphabet from A to Z.

7 On the seventh day of kindergarten,
my teacher gave to me
SEVEN stacks for sorting,

six fish for feeding,

five gold stars!

Four puzzle shapes,

three pencils,

two picture books,

and the whole alphabet from A to Z.

On the eighth day of kindergarten,

my teacher gave to me

EIGHT beads for stringing,

seven stacks for sorting,

six fish for feeding,

five gold stars!

Four puzzle shapes,

three pencils,

two picture books,

and the whole alphabet from A to Z.

9 On the ninth day of kindergarten,
my teacher gave to me
NINE blocks for building,
eight beads for stringing,
seven stacks for sorting,
six fish for feeding,
five gold stars!
Four puzzle shapes,
three pencils,
two picture books,
and the whole alphabet from A to Z.

10 On the tenth day of kindergarten,
my teacher gave to me
TEN coins for counting,
nine blocks for building,
eight beads for stringing,
seven stacks for sorting,
six fish for feeding,
five gold stars!
Four puzzle shapes,
three pencils,
two picture books,
and the whole alphabet
from A to Z.

Children's Museum

11

On the eleventh day of kindergarten,
my teacher gave to me
ELEVEN seeds for planting,
ten coins for counting,
nine blocks for building,
eight beads for stringing,
seven stacks for sorting,
six fish for feeding,
five gold stars!
Four puzzle shapes,
three pencils,
two picture books,
and the whole alphabet from A to Z.

12 On the twelfth day of kindergarten,
my teacher gave to me
TWELVE eggs for hatching,
eleven seeds for planting,
ten coins for counting,
nine blocks for building,
eight beads for stringing,
seven stacks for sorting,
six fish for feeding

five gold stars!
Four puzzle shapes,
three pencils,
two picture books,

and the whole alphabet from A to Z!

Oo Pp Qq Rr Ss Tt Uu Vv Ww Xx Yy Zz

pink green
red blue
yellow brown

CHOOL

Cataloging-in-Publication Data has been applied for and may be obtained
from the Library of Congress.

Paperback ISBN 978-1-4197-2742-9

Originally published in hardcover by Abrams Books for Young Readers in 2003

Printed and bound in China
10 9 8 7 6 5 4 3 2 1

Abrams Books for Young Readers are available at special discounts when purchased
in quantity for premiums and promotions as well as fundraising or educational use.
Special editions can also be created to specification.
For details, contact specialsales@abramsbooks.com or the address below.

ABRAMS The Art of Books
115 West 18th Street, New York, NY 10011
abramsbooks.com